THIS BOOK BELONGS TO

....

....

BEDTIME STORIES FOR EVERY DAY

Inspirational and Calming Stories For Toddlers and Children To Fall Asleep

Mary A. Cardigan

CONTENTS

A BOY WHO ALWAYS WENT 'BUMP!' AND HOW HIS FRIENDS HELPED HIM

Alan was a little boy who always went 'Bump!' He had a lovely smile and a big round face, and everyone loved him. And because Alan was so kind, no one minded when he bumped into things. It was just who Alan was, and they loved him for it.

One day, Alan was getting ready for school and his mum could see how excited he was. When she asked Alan why he was so excited, he told her all about the new boy who would be joining his class.

Alan loved it when someone new joined his class because it meant he could show them around. He loved to make new friends and meet new people, which is why his teacher always got the new children to sit right next to Alan.

Before his mum could finish telling him what a lovely little boy he was, he was grinning by the front door. He had finished his toast, made his lunch, and even managed to find his coat. She was so proud of her lovely little boy.

Alan ran down the drive and jumped into the car. He bounced up and down in his seat with excitement. He knew he was going to make a new friend today, and he was so happy about it.

When Alan got to school, he kissed his mum goodbye and ran into the classroom. He saw his teacher talking to a new boy at the front of the class. It must be the new boy everyone was told about yesterday, which would mean he would be sitting next to Alan.

Soon, the boy was sitting beside Alan. He was shy and quiet, but Alan didn't mind. He just wanted to make a new friend and have lots of fun.

For the rest of the morning, the boy hardly said a word. Every time Alan asked him something, he'd go red and feel shy, but that was okay. Alan knew it must be difficult being the new kid in a big school.

When it got to lunchtime, Alan invited the boy to go outside and play. At first, he didn't seem to want to leave his chair or talk to Alan, but that all changed when he heard they were playing football. The boy started talking excitedly and bouncing up and down, ready to play football.

In the playground, Alan saw straight away that the new boy was amazing at football. He could score with both feet and run faster and tackle better than anyone else in the school. It was so nice to see his new friend having fun and smiling, and Alan couldn't have been happier for him.

After he'd finished his snacks, Alan decided to join in. He wasn't very good at football, but that didn't stop him from loving to play. He missed the ball a couple of times, and soon the new boy was running straight at him, trying to score the winning goal. Alan stuck out his foot, and everyone stopped when they heard a really big 'Bump!'

Alan was a little bit clumsy, so everyone was used to it. Except the new boy. He jumped up with a big red face and a sore knee. He was shouting at Alan, calling him names, and he even looked like he was about to push him over. Someone had to do something...

Tom was the goalie at the other end of the pitch. Because he was such good friends with Alan, he ran as fast as he could and stood between Alan and the new boy. He wanted to make sure his friend was okay, so he started to calm the new boy down.

Tom told him that Alan was a little bit clumsy and he couldn't really help it. Alan would never do anything to hurt the new boy or to cheat, so the new boy should stay friends with Alan. The only problem was he was so angry that it looked like nothing would work...

But soon he started to calm down. His face went pink again, and he looked at Alan, who looked really sad. They carried on playing for the rest of lunchtime, but as they went back inside, something amazing happened...

The new boy ran over to Alan and gave him a really big, warm cuddle. He told Alan he was sorry for getting so cross and that he now knew Alan couldn't help it. Then the new boy asked Alan if he pushed him over to make fun of his squeaky voice...

Alan was confused. He hadn't even noticed the boy's voice. The boy was amazed because everyone at his old school had made fun of him about it!

As they walked into the classroom, they were laughing and joking about it all. They chatted while they did their work for the rest of the day and then asked their parents if they could have tea together. Their parents agreed, delighted that their lovely little boys had made a new friend.

Alan and the new boy also asked Tom's mum if he could come over and play later, and she said she would bring him in the car after he'd had his tea.

As Tom's mum drove home, she looked in the back at her little boy. Tom was smiling and looking quietly out of the window. When she asked him who his new friends were, he just kept on smiling.

She knew she had a very kind and loving little boy. Tom knew he had a great friend in Alan and a new friend who was amazing at football. And everyone in the class knew how brave and kind Tom was for helping the new boy when no one else knew what to do.

A MONSTER WHO WAS SCARED OF THE DARK AND NEEDED A FRIEND

Zack was a big, scary, hairy, loud monster who was amazing at making people jump. He knew how to make kids jump, how to make grown-ups jump, and even how to make other monsters jump. There was no one he couldn't scare, which was why he knew he had to keep his little secret...

Because Zack was so scary, everyone thought there was nothing he was scared of, but there was one thing. Zack did all of his scaring and tricks in the daytime — a strange time for a monster — because he had a little secret.

Everyone thought his daytime scaring was the secret to him being such an amazing monster, but there was something they didn't know: Zack was afraid of the dark.

When the sun went down and the moon came out, Zack always felt scared. Even though he was big, scary, and hairy, he knew that anyone could be hiding in the dark. The problem was no one would believe he was scared of anything because he was so scary.

One day, Zack was busy scaring people in the park. He wanted to try to beat his record for scaring old people in one day, which meant he was out for a very long time.

When Zack finally broke his record and looked at his wrist, he realised he'd forgotten his watch! He had no idea what time it was, which meant the sun might be going down soon!

He didn't want anyone to see him scared after dark, so he started running to get the bus home. The bus? Could a monster as scary as Zack ever get the bus without getting into trouble? He had no idea, but he tried to get on it anyway.

When the bus pulled up, the driver took one look at Zack's hairy arms and giant teeth, closed the door, and drove away. Zack really was super-scary, but it wasn't helping him right then! He needed to get home, but he had no idea how to get help from anyone because he kept scaring them away. Even when he tried his very best not to look scary, he was just too big for anyone to relax enough to help him.

It was no use. Zack would have to try to get home by himself and do his best not to be scared. Most of the sunshine had left the sky and big black clouds were blocking the moonlight. It was like a nightmare for Zack — he couldn't let anyone find out that this big scary monster was actually super-scared of the dark himself! How would he ever be able to scare anyone ever again if they knew just how scared he was right then?

As the sun kept getting lower in the sky, Zack decided he had to start running. He thought that he would be able to get home so much faster by running, but he was just too big to run very far. In less than a few minutes, he was so tired he could barely move another step.

Before he knew it, Zack was sitting on a bench, shaking because he was so scared. The running had made him really tired, and the time of day had made the sky really dark. There were big, scary, black shadows everywhere, and each one of them made Zack want to cry.

He knew he wasn't going to be able to get home, and he knew he would never be able to scare anyone again. Who would be scared by a monster who got so scared? He was also really hungry and could hear his tummy rumbling. Zack just didn't know what to do, so he let out a loud cry and curled up on the ground. He closed his eyes and hoped that everything would be okay. But something was soon bothering him...

Zack could feel some little fingers tickling one of his big feet. He thought it was really odd because he didn't have little fingers — his fingers were like big, fat sausages. When Zack looked up, he saw that his big feet were being tickled by a little girl. She was giggling and having lots of fun with the cute little monster she'd found.

When Zack got up, she saw he was actually a giant monster who was so super-scary, but something stopped her from running away. She could see that Zack had been crying, and she wanted to know why.

She gently asked him if something was wrong, when had it happened, and would he like to talk about it. They were really kind and gentle questions to ask someone, especially a big scary monster like Zack. He couldn't believe how lovely she was being to him and thanked her from the bottom of his heart. Then she did something that made Zack smile...

She held out her tiny hand and said she would walk him home. Even if it took until dinner time, she would be by his side, showing him that being scared of the dark was normal. There were so many people out there who were afraid of the dark and never went out after dark that she'd stopped trying to count them. What was really important was that Zack saw that nothing would happen.

The little girl made sure that Zack knew she was always there for him. That let him walk with a smile on his face, and he saw that nothing was hiding in the shadows. After all, if a little girl could walk through the shadows, a big, scary monster definitely could.

And do you know the best bit?

The best bit is that the little girl never asked Zack for anything in return, and she never made jokes about how scared he used to be. All she wanted was to show the monster that it was okay to be scared.

When you're scared, you can ask someone to help you and they'll do it without making fun of you, just like the little girl did to help Zack!

THE LITTLE GIRL WHO SHARED HER LAST SNACK TO MAKE SOMEONE SMILE

Alice was a kind little girl who always loved to make other people happy. She knew that if she could make just one person smile, she could help them to do amazing things whenever they wanted to. But Alice wasn't always busy making people smile. Her other favourite thing to do was to eat tasty snacks.

Whenever she opened up a new bag of snacks, she counted them when no one was looking. She wanted to know how many she had so she could really enjoy every single one of them. Eating snacks in secret was her favourite thing to do, but she didn't always get away with it.

One day, Alice was walking in the park. She was putting her hand into her pocket to get another sweet snack when she saw something amazing. There was a little boy who was amazing at running. He was beating all of his friends in a race, and it wasn't even close. She couldn't believe how good at running he was.

When he got near the finish line, he started celebrating and waving his arms in the air. That was a big mistake! Bang! He fell down and hit his knees really hard on the path. The path was rough and hard, not like the grass at all. He started rolling on the floor, crying and holding his knees, and saying he wanted to go home.

Just when Alice thought his friends were going to help him, they jumped over him and won the race. They'd never beaten him, so they were all so excited. Soon, they forgot all about him and started to play football in a different part of the park. Alice knew they were excited, but how could they leave their friend when he was crying so much? What could she do to help him?

Alice shut her eyes and thought really hard. Then she had a bright idea. She could go and help the boy up and ask him if he was okay. Then he would know someone cared about him and would run off to play with his friends.

She walked over, smiled, and held out her little hand. As the boy dried his tears, he looked up and saw Alice smiling down at him. He had never met her before, but he knew he could trust her. Alice had such a cute little face that everyone knew how nice she was the moment they met her.

The boy reached for Alice's hand, but he didn't get up. He told her that his knees were too sore and that he really wanted someone to sit with him until he felt better. Alice was on her way to the shop to get more snacks, so she didn't want to stop. But she was also very kind, so she knew she had to sit with him!

She sat down, stretched out her legs, and listened quietly while the boy talked. He told her how he was really upset that all his friends had jumped over him instead of checking if he was okay. He thought they were all great friends, so why had they acted like that? Alice didn't know the answer right then, so she closed her eyes and thought really hard. Soon, she had another bright idea!

Alice told the boy that his friends still liked him. It was just that they never got to beat him in a race. They loved him and were proud of how fast he could run, but they were also a little bit jealous sometimes. When they saw the chance to beat him, they took it and had some fun. Maybe it was a little bit naughty, but it wasn't nasty or mean. They were still friends!

The boy started to dry his eyes some more and then showed Alice a little smile. His smile had been hiding ever since he'd fallen down, so it was nice for it to appear in front of Alice.

He then told her all about how his knees really hurt and he thought he would have to get his mum and dad to carry him home. That was when Alice decided to do something she had never done before: she shared her last snack with someone.

She reached into her pocket, pulled out the sweet treat, and broke it in half with her fingers. The boy smiled and licked his lips as he enjoyed every bit of his half. Alice used to think she would cry if she lost some of her treats, but she didn't feel like she'd lost this one. She knew she was doing something to make someone else happy. It was a really great feeling and one that made her very happy.

They sat talking while the other boys played in the other bit of the park. Suddenly, a dog ran past and grabbed Alice's hat from the ground. She had put it down when she'd sat down next to the boy. She really loved her hat, but she knew there was no way she'd be able to catch such a fast dog. She closed her eyes and started to cry.

Before she knew it, something amazing happened. The boy tapped her on the shoulder and gave her back the hat. Had he given her a hat that looked exactly the same? No! This hat even had her name tag inside. How had he done it?

The boy told her how he had chased the dog, caught it, and tickled its tummy until it gave him back her hat. He hadn't even noticed his knees didn't hurt anymore!

It just goes to show what happens when you're kind to someone you don't know...

AN AMAZING RACING CAR THAT ANYONE COULD DRIVE ANYWHERE

Everyone in Cuddle Town knew about the big red racing car. It was fast, quick, and never lost a race. The best thing about it was that you didn't have to be a grown-up to drive it — the car would let anyone drive it, as long as they were kind to everyone they met that day.

One day, Max was on his way to school with two of his friends, Simon and Lucy. The three of them knew a shortcut through a farmer's field, and they took it whenever they were late or it was raining and they wanted to get inside nice and quick.

As they climbed over the fence into the field, they saw that the gate on the other side of the field was broken. Someone had left it hanging off and all the cows and sheep were escaping. The farmer must have had no idea because he was always in town buying food in the mornings. When he got home, he wouldn't have any animals to look after because they would have walked away through the broken gate.

Max asked his two friends if they could help him fix the gate, but they both just laughed at him. When he asked again, they told him that they didn't care about the farmer's animals, they just wanted to get to school on time and miss the thunderstorm. When Max took off his bag and said he wouldn't walk with them, they didn't even turn around. Lucy and Simon went to school while Max stood there wondering what to do.

He knew that the animals were special and they were really cared for by the farmer. The farmer had had them for years and years, and it would be impossible for him to find all of them. Even worse than that, some of them might get injured or hurt themselves by walking into the road. Max knew he had to do something to help the farmer and to help save his lovely animals.

He picked up his bag, ran to the other side of the field, and looked up at the sky. The thunderstorm had just started, and the rain was coming down heavily. Before Max knew it, he was soaked and covered in mud. He was also really late for school by now, but he knew that he had to keep the animals safe before the farmer got back.

When he got to the gate, he saw something that made him very happy. The gate wasn't broken after all, it was just left wide open. Max used all his strength to close the gate. It was so big, heavy, and old, that it was really hard to move it. Max kept trying and, little by little, he closed the gate.

After a very long time and lots of brave pushing, Max shut the gate and sat down to rest under a big tree. The rain was getting heavier and heavier, but Max didn't care. He knew he had done something really important by closing the gate. He nearly fell asleep because he was so tired, but then something made him jump!

He could see that the gate wouldn't stay closed because it was too windy. All of his hard work had been for nothing, which meant he had to come up with another bright idea. It was the only way to help the farmer and keep all of his lovely animals safe.

Max thought long and hard about what to do, and he suddenly came up with a wonderful idea! He had some string for an art project in his bag. He took a big piece of it, wrapped it around his hand, and pulled as hard as he could. The string was so strong that it didn't break at all, not even a tiny little bit! This was amazing and exactly what he needed to make sure the gate stayed shut, even when it was really windy.

As he ran towards the gate, he felt braver and stronger than he had the first time. He knew he could push it and close it, and now he knew exactly how he was going to keep it closed. It took a long time to close the gate, but Max got there in the end. He was so proud when he saw the gate closed with the strong string. He didn't even care that his school uniform was so wet and muddy that it looked like it was about to fall apart. All he cared about was that no more lovely animals could escape.

Max knew everything would be okay until the farmer came home. He picked up his school bag and went home. He couldn't go to school like this! That was when something really amazing happened...

As he climbed back over the fence and down onto the road, the red car came zooming up the street. It was smiling at him and telling him how brave and kind he had been. Max couldn't believe the car already knew, so he gave it the biggest, warmest smile anyone had ever seen.

The car then opened its door and said a couple of magic spells. When Max closed the door, he noticed he was wearing a perfectly clean and dry uniform, ready for school. The car started spinning, and he saw the clock turning backwards. What was going on?

Max asked the car, and the car told him it wasn't just a car anyone could drive, it was a magic car. It was travelling back in time so Max wouldn't be late. Max couldn't believe how magical it was, and he enjoyed every second of the ride.

As the car pulled up to the school gates, Lucy and Simon were amazed to see Max in it because no one they knew had ever been inside. When they asked him how he'd found the car, he told them that good things always have a habit of finding kind people.

THE SPARKLING STARFISH WHO HAD TO BE BRAVE

Sara was a sparkling starfish that everyone in the sea knew about. She had amazing sparkly skin that constantly changed colour and made everyone she met smile. No one knew how she did it because her mum and dad were just normal starfish. They had bright colours and kind faces, but they never changed colour. Sara's parents were always the same colour, which made her very special indeed.

When Sara changed colour, she was the star of the show and everyone would look at her and smile. It was an amazing talent that she had, and everyone seemed to be really happy for her. After all, it's lovely to have a talent that makes someone smile.

After a long day at school, Alice asked her mum if she could have a little rest. Her mum said she could, but she had to do one job first. She had to go to the shop to pick up some tomato sauce for dinner. Starfish love family meals, and they especially love things like tomato sauce, so Alice didn't mind at all. She put on her hat, put on all five of her shoes, and swam out the door on her way to the shop.

As she swam through the village, she sped across the roads and whizzed around the corners. She loved swimming nice and fast like this, and she could see her sparkling skin popping up in all the windows. It was like Christmas lights that made everyone smile, and she was so proud to be the one who made it possible. But then suddenly, something scary happened...

Too big grumpy fish swam out from under a rock. One was very red and very fat, and one was a little bit longer and a little bit blue. They were both looking really rather angry and definitely didn't want to be friends with Sara. She was used to people smiling and being nice to her, so she had no idea what to do next. When she tried to make them smile by showing them her sparkly skin, they both started shouting at her.

When they stopped shouting, they swam away in a big huff, leaving Sara to cry. She was still a long way from the shop and because she was closer to home, she decided to go and hide in her bedroom. It was the one place in the world where everyone was sparkly, which is why she wanted to hide there more than anything in the whole world.

As Sara quietly opened the door and swam upstairs, hardly anyone in the house noticed. After all, they'd expected her to be so much longer and to tell them when she was back.

After nearly an hour, Sara's mum noticed that the tomato sauce still hadn't arrived and started to worry. She turned off the TV, closed the kitchen door, and started putting on her coat so she could go out and look for Sara. Because everything was so quiet, she could hear everything in the house, which meant she heard Sara crying upstairs. She was really worried because it wasn't like Sara to cry, especially after sneaking back into the house without coming to talk to anyone.

Sara's mum swam upstairs and knocked gently on the door. When Sara opened it, her mum saw that she'd been crying; crying an awful lot of big tears. She asked Sara what was wrong and how it was making her feel. She also asked if anyone was being mean to her and why she thought that was. When Sara told her all about the two grumpy, angry fish she had never seen before, her mum knew exactly who she was talking about.

She told Sara that Spencer and Louise were always trying to be mean to people because they were actually very unhappy fish. They didn't like it when someone else was happy, good at something, or even making new friends because they couldn't do any of those things. She told Sara not to worry about what fish like that said to her and that she would help her get to the shop. Sara was very nervous, but she decided to be extra brave and follow her mum. At least she could make sure Sara was safe and protected if the angry fish got even angrier.

As they swam out the door and raced towards the rock where Spencer and Louise lived, Sara started to feel even braver. She knew her sparkly starfish body was very special, and she knew that Spencer and Louise were just being jealous. She also knew that her mum would be there to protect her and keep her safe.

Sara was getting so brave that she swam a little bit ahead, which turned out to be a great idea. Spencer and Louise jumped straight out from behind the rock and started to make fun of her. They told her how her sparkly skin was silly and how all the other fish only pretended to like her. Sara thought she might cry again, but then her mum appeared right next to her.

When her mum told Spencer and Louise to say sorry, they both went very quiet and looked at the floor. After a little bit more quiet time, they said sorry and swam away very slowly. In fact, they were so sorry that no one saw them for the rest of the day. When they did come back out, they started to smile at people.

How had her mum done it? She had shown Sara that good things happen and you can do anything when you are brave.

THE LITTLE FISH WHO COULDN'T SWIM

Billy was a little fish who couldn't swim. He was very round and had tiny little flippers, which made it very hard for him to swim, no matter how hard he tried. Every other fish in his class could swim just fine. They were fish, after all.

One day, Billy's big brother decided to help Billy swim. As they were walking to school, Johnny asked Billy why he thought he couldn't swim. Billy told him all about how his body was too big and round and his flippers were too small and short. No fish would be able to swim when they were shaped like Billy, so he knew he'd never be able to swim. In fact, Billy said it so many times that Johnny started to think he might be right.

But Johnny couldn't let his little brother down, so he decided to think of new ways to help him. He thought really hard about why Billy knew he couldn't swim. How did he know? How could he be so sure? He had never really tried to swim and trying was what really mattered when you wanted to learn to swim. This gave Johnny a really bright idea!

That evening, he opened up the family computer and showed Billy videos of the fastest fish in the world. They were famous because they could swim faster than even the fastest sharks, and they won so many medals and trophies for swimming so fast. Billy knew all about these fish, of course — everyone did. Then Johnny loaded up some videos of some very small, slow, strange-looking fish. They were round with short flippers and they were really not getting anywhere in the water. It would have been so much quicker for them to walk, but they stayed thrashing around in the water. Why was Johnny showing this video to Billy?

Billy thought Johnny was trying to make fun of him for being a very bad swimmer, because that was what everyone else did. Then he realised that his big brother never made fun of him, so there had to be another reason for showing him this video. What on earth could it be?

Johnny asked him to look at the names of the little fish and the answer amazed Billy! They had the same names as the super-fast fish in the first video. What an amazing bit of luck to be named after such fast fish! Or was it...?

Johnny told Billy that the video was of the first few times the super-fast fish had ever swum. They were very young in this old video, but it showed Billy everyone has to start somewhere. These super-fast fish that Billy, and the rest of the ocean, loved so much weren't born fast. They had to work hard and practice. And some of them started off rounder and with even shorter flippers than Billy!

This was amazing because it showed Billy that he could learn to swim if he believed he could. Some of the fastest fish in the whole ocean had started just like him, and look at them now! They were so fast that not even the fastest shark could catch them in a race. What if Billy could be as fast as one of them one day?

Johnny started to smile because he could see that his little brother was starting to get it. If he believed he could do something, then it may very well happen. But if he told himself it would never happen, he would always prove himself right. It was like a superpower for Billy because it soon allowed him to do things he never thought possible. In just one week, he was doing full lengths of the swimming pool at school. He was very slow and getting very tired, but he was actually swimming all by himself!

In another couple of weeks, he could catch the slowest fish in the class and he couldn't believe how he'd done it. Then, by the end of the year, he was able to catch all but three of the very fastest fish in the whole school. The amazing thing was that when he became one of the fastest fish himself, everyone talked like he had been born super-fast. That was when something really important happened...

Eric was a new fish in school and wanted to be on the swimming team. The problem was that although he could swim, he was tiny and kept getting lost in the swimming pool. Eric wanted to be on the team so badly that he started talking to the three fastest fish in the school about how they didn't get lost, but they just made fun of him. That was when Billy decided he was going to help Eric, just like Johnny had helped him.

Billy told the fish how he'd been a round little fish with short little flippers, and how he'd figured out how to swim really fast. He also came up with a plan that Eric could practice every day so he wouldn't get lost in the swimming pool at school. The amazing thing was that because such a fast fish was telling all this to Eric, he tried extra hard and did incredibly well.

By the end of the week, Eric could do a whole length without getting lost. By the end of the month, he was twice the size because the swimming had helped him grow super-fast. And by the end of the term, he was the next fish to join the school swimming team.

By that point, Billy had become the captain and all the fish knew they could come to him for help. It was all set to be a school year they would never forget!

THE DINOSAUR WITH THE BIG WOBBLY TOOTH

Rex was a dinosaur with big, sharp teeth. Everywhere he went, people would look at his teeth and be amazed. They were big, white, and ever so sharp, but there was also something strange about Rex's teeth.

At the front, Rex had one big wobbly tooth that was really sore. Sometimes, he felt like he wanted to cry. Other times, he wished it would just fall out. But no matter what Rex did, his tooth just ached and wobbled and never came out. It was really annoying, and he knew he'd have to find a way to get it out.

When Rex woke up one day, he looked at his alarm clock and saw it was time to get ready for school. Rex loved school because he could see all of his friends, eat tasty snacks at lunchtime, and learn lots of amazing things. School was the bit of the day he always looked forward to, so he jumped out of bed and ran downstairs.

His mum gave him a big pile of dino toast, and he ate it very carefully, making sure not to knock his wobbly tooth. Every time he bit something with it, it really hurt. The last thing he wanted to do was cry about his tooth before he even got to school!

Rex finished his toast, drank all his dino juice, and got ready to brush all of his big teeth. When he got to his wobbly tooth, he was extra careful and very gentle. He didn't want to knock it, so he took his time and made sure it was nice and clean. Hopefully, it would fall out soon!

On his way to school, Rex loved to look out of the window. His mum was driving, and he was daydreaming. He was trying to put his big wobbly tooth out of his mind and look forward to school. Before he knew it, he was walking up the school gates, saying funny jokes to everyone he met. Because Rex was such a funny dino, everyone loved it when he sat at their table for lunch. But before lunch, there was some learning to do...

Rex walked through the door and hung up his bag. When he sat down, he saw they were going to do maths all morning. Rex thought he might cry because his tooth was really hurting and maths was the only subject he didn't like. Well, that wasn't quite true. Rex really wanted to like maths, but he found it so hard. And when you find something very hard, it's easy to make yourself think you don't like it.

When Stego sat down next to him, Rex started to feel better. Stego was so clever when it came to maths that he always tried to help Rex. The problem was that no matter how hard he tried, it never seemed to work out. Rex also had the problem of his wobbly tooth, which was really starting to bother him.

Stego saw that Rex was about to cry and started to talk to him about maths. He told him that he would get top marks if he just copied his answers, but it wouldn't help him next time. He also told him how he had become so good at maths: lots and lots of practice.

This really surprised Rex because he thought you were either born good at maths or born bad at maths. Stego told him how he practiced maths every evening with his mum and dad, and how he thought that was why he was always top of the class. Rex didn't quite believe him, so Stego gave him an example.

In football, Rex was one of the best. He played every night after his dinner, and because he was good at it, he wanted to play even more. Stego was really bad at football and he never really played either. Rex started to see that with practice, he could get as good at maths as Stego.

He decided to really focus on what Stego was telling him so that he would find maths easier next time. It was going to be hard today, but it would get easier tomorrow, and that made it something really worth doing. So Rex tried and tried and tried, and then he tried a whole lot more all over again. It was really tiring for his brain, but it was also making him quite happy — he could feel himself getting better. Then, just before lunch, something amazing happened: he got three right answers in a row! He'd never done that!

When the lunch bell rang, Rex and Stego went outside for their lunch. Rex had a giant ham sandwich while Stego had a little salad. The fact they were so different in so many ways was what made them friends. Rex normally loved lunch, but because of his tooth, he was a bit scared of it. He took a tiny bite — not his normal giant bite — and didn't feel a thing. Finally, he had found an easier way to eat with that annoying wobbly tooth!

Rex spent the whole of lunchtime taking tiny bite after tiny bite, but he finally finished his sandwich. When he got back to his desk, he felt a bit sad that he'd not had time to play. Then suddenly he saw something shining underneath his desk...

It was the wobbly tooth! How had it got all the way down there? How hadn't he noticed it?

Stego told him he had heard it drop out when they were doing maths. Rex was thinking so hard he hadn't noticed. Stego hadn't wanted to disturb him, and Rex hadn't felt a thing.

They laughed about how you can do just about anything when you try really hard at something; even get rid of a wobbly tooth without feeling a thing...

THE PENGUIN WHO WAS ALWAYS FALLING OVER

Steve the penguin loved to run around on the ice, the only problem was he was terrible on his feet. He couldn't swim — the water was far too cold — so he ran around instead. The polar bears always let him play football with them because they wanted him to be happy, but there was no way Steve could score a goal unless they let him...

After another game of football where Steve spent half of the time falling over and the other half getting back up, he headed home. His friend Snowy the bear was with him and was trying to make him feel a bit happier about the game. Steve loved football. He just couldn't play it very well. His little feet were fine for walking, but not for running. The bears were big and tall, steady and strong, but Steve just kept falling over.

Snowy tried to tell Steve that it was okay not to be very good at something, as long as you enjoyed it anyway. No one could be great at everything, but Steve didn't seem to be very good at any sports. He'd tried rugby, hockey, and tennis and he had the same problem every time — he was always falling over. He'd even asked his granddad for some new boots for Christmas, but they didn't work either. Maybe Steve was just bad at every kind of sport.

At the shop, Steve and Snowy got a bottle of pop and some ice cakes to share. They loved sharing because it made them both feel really happy. When they finished eating their snacks, they jumped back to their feet and carried on home. On the way, they saw some of the really big polar bears playing football and they stopped to watch. The bears were so big and fast that Steve couldn't believe it. If only he was a bear, he'd be able to play that well. Could he become a bear? He couldn't think of a way to make it happen, so he started to daydream.

After what seemed like a very long time, Steve woke up with a start. The polar bears were all shouting and pushing each other. What had Steve missed? Snowy told him one of the biggest bears had kicked the ball so hard it had been blown into the ocean by the wind. Polar bears like Snowy and the football players could swim a little, but the ball was drifting away so fast that they'd never be able to catch it. The worst bit was that it was their only ball, and it was a really important game of football.

One of the big bears called Steve's name, but Steve just stood there, daydreaming again. Suddenly, he saw Fluffy, the biggest bear in the village, standing over him and smiling. Had Steve done something wrong? Fluffy was one of his heroes because of how good he was at football. Steve didn't know what to do or say because he was so excited.

Fluffy asked him if he could swim after the ball and bring it back. Steve told him he couldn't swim because he'd heard the water was too cold. He also told him how he always fell over and how that meant he'd be really bad at every new sport he tried. Fluffy looked a little bit confused because he knew something Steve didn't: penguins are amazing swimmers, even if they've never done it before. Fluffy also knew that penguins never felt the cold in the water because their feathers and fur were perfect for keeping them warm.

Steve was so amazed to have his hero talking to him that he listened when Fluffy told him he was a great swimmer. He couldn't let Fluffy down, so he started to feel brave and to tell himself he really could do it. Fluffy came to the edge of the ice with him and stood there cheering for him the whole way. Steve jumped into the water, didn't feel a thing, and got the ball back to Fluffy in record time. How was it even possible?

As Steve climbed back onto the ice, he slipped a little bit. Fluffy gave him a big hug. He told Steve that it didn't matter if he wasn't very good at football because everyone was great at different things. He also told Steve that just because he was bad at football didn't mean he couldn't get better with practice, or that he should stop playing it. If you enjoy something and you practice it, you will always get better. Fluffy even told him that he used to be very average at football. He was never bad, but he definitely wasn't born the best player in the village.

Steve was so happy to have Fluffy making him feel confident about football that he couldn't believe it. He also knew something he hadn't known that morning — he was an excellent swimmer!

Swimming suddenly became really interesting to Steve because he saw just how good he was already. If he practiced swimming as hard as he practiced dribbling with the football, he might even be able to win races against the other animals in the village. Imagine that!

Over the next few weeks, Steve swam every day after school, getting faster and faster each time. Before long, no one mentioned it when he slipped over during football matches. What they talked about was how he'd won so many medals and trophies for coming first in the village swimming races. He was no longer the penguin who always fell over, he was the penguin who could beat anyone in the village at swimming!

THE OCTOPUS WHO WAS IN A REAL MUDDLE

Ollie had eight legs, two big eyes, and no bones. That meant he could swim fast, see far, and fit into the tiniest gaps when he was playing hide and seek. But Ollie also got scared and squirted his ink sometimes. He was supposed to use it to swim away and get safe, but he always got in a real muddle. No matter how hard he tried, he could never figure out where to go or how to stop squirting so much ink.

When Ollie was on his way to school, he saw a big angry fish who always jumped out and scared him. He was so used to it that he squirted his ink and ran without even waiting for the fish to scare him. Bang!

What was that?

Ollie had no idea how it had happened, but he had swum into a giant rock and hit his head. It was hurting and really sore, which was no good because he had an important maths test later. How would he be able to figure out all the sums and hard questions when his head was hurting so much? It didn't seem possible...

When Ollie's ink had gone away and he could see again, he started to figure out where he was. He was still two turns away from school, which means he was still going to get there in time. On his way, he spotted Chuckles who was one of his best friends. Chuckles was a friendly clownish who was able to make anyone laugh about anything.

On their way into school, they told jokes, had lots of laughs, and started to talk about the really important maths test. It was so important that Ollie was really worried about it because his head was so painful. No matter how hard he tried not to, he couldn't stop thinking about his sore head. He told Chuckles he was worried and that he thought he would have to tell the teacher he needed to go home.

Chuckles loved his friend very much and knew how nervous Ollie would get if he had to wait even longer to do the test. He'd been studying really hard to make sure he could pass, so having to wait to do it by himself didn't seem fair. Then Chuckles came up with a really clever idea: Ollie could use his eight wiggly arms to help him count. Ollie thought this was a crazy idea because surely you needed to use your brain to do maths, not your arms.

Because they were such great friends, Ollie listened to Chuckles even though he didn't think his crazy new idea would work. It took a couple of minutes for Chuckles to explain everything, which Ollie thought meant Chuckles was just making all of it up. The good news was that he wasn't!

Chuckles gave Ollie a simple sum to do using his eight wiggly arms and watched Ollie do it with ease. He wasn't in a muddle — he was making maths look very easy. Ollie couldn't believe it either because it meant that he was learning a new skill very fast indeed. When the test was over, Ollie gave Chuckles one of his chocolate biscuits and a big hug. He couldn't have done any of this without his friend. Ollie also started to think about other ways he could get himself out of muddles.

He asked Chuckles about what he should do when he squirted ink everywhere and got confused. Chuckles didn't have any ink of his own, so Ollie thought he would tell him to ask someone else. But Chuckles was a very kind and caring fish and a very loyal friend. He sat thinking for a little bit and then started to smile. He had come up with a new idea...

Chuckles told Ollie that he was getting in a muddle because he was squirting his ink and then trying to swim. What would happen if he did things the other way round? What if he started to swim, just a tiny little bit, and then squirted his ink? Ollie sat there and thought about it for a little bit.

He soon started to see why Chuckles had asked him to do it that way. If he was already swimming, the ink would stay in a big cloud behind him, not a cloud that covered him. The person who was scaring him wouldn't be able to see him, but Ollie would be able to see exactly where he was going. It was really clever, but the answer had only come because Ollie had listened to someone. Chuckles knew nothing about firing ink himself, but that didn't mean he couldn't say something useful.

Ollie thanked Chuckles for telling him so many helpful things, and Chuckles gave him a big smile. In the future, Ollie would be able to do his maths tests easier, get away when someone scared him, and generally avoid getting in a big muddle. The best bit was he'd learned simple ways to do all of these things just by listening to his best friend.

When Ollie got home, he told his dad all about the things he learned. His dad was really very proud. He told Ollie that it was really important to listen to everyone, not just the people who were just like you. Chuckles was very different from the octopuses Ollie knew, which was one of the reasons why he had completely new ideas.

It just goes to show how you can learn something amazing and make yourself very happy just by finding some new ideas. And the best place to find new ideas? Sometimes, it's from the people (or fish) you think are very different from yourself.

THE CLOCK THAT TICKED REALLY LOUDLY

Paul lived in a big house with his mum and dad. His parents were busy people who were always working, buying Paul new toys, and then working some more in the evening. Sometimes, they'd even work at the dinner table while Paul was finishing his dessert. Paul didn't mind, but sometimes he wished he could have a bit more of a cuddle with his mum, or a wrestling match with his dad. But it was okay, Paul was very loved and also had a lot of shiny new toys.

One thing that wasn't shiny and new in their house was the clock in the hallway. It was a big wooden grandfather clock that his mum and dad said was over 100 years old. They had spent a lot of money on it and were very proud of it. The clock was cleaned once a week, never knocked or scratched, and always told exactly the right time. The clock truly was perfect. But Paul didn't think so...

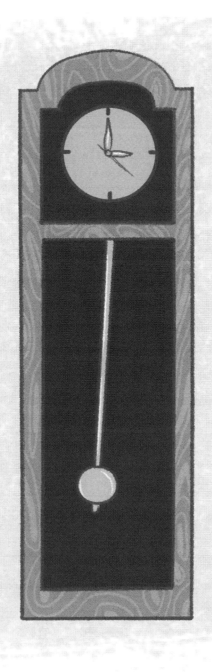

His bedroom was right above the clock, which meant he could hear it ticking and tocking all night long. At first, it didn't bother Paul because he knew the clock was really important to his mum and dad. But sure enough, the ticking always seemed louder during the night, which made it very hard for Paul to sleep. He told his mum and dad that he thought there was something wrong with the clock, but they told him to leave it alone, not worry, and come down for some snacks if he couldn't sleep.

One night, Paul was being kept wide awake by the ticking and tocking, so he decided to listen to his dad's advice and started heading downstairs to get a nighttime snack. He walked down the stairs, around the corner, and past the clock. When he got to the kitchen, he flicked on the light and saw something really surprising. The clock was walking into the kitchen!

Suddenly, Paul looked at the clock and saw that it also had a face. It had been a magical clock for all these years and no one had noticed. How had no one noticed the clock was so special? The truth was that, because it was also right in front of them, his parents just didn't notice it. If it had been brand new, they would have probably paid it more attention.

The clock began to speak and asked Paul why everyone had been ignoring it. The clock even said it would tick very loudly at night in the hope that someone would come downstairs and talk to it. Its magic only worked after bedtime, but it needed a human to make a wish so it could do its magic. Without a human downstairs, all it could do was tick and tock and try to wake someone up. Now that Paul was downstairs, it could impress him with some amazing magic.

The clock created bubbles and rainbows that floated around Paul's head and made him very happy. Next, it played the most amazing type of music Paul had ever heard. It was magical music that allowed him to do anything he wanted. One moment he wanted to fly, and he was flying. The next moment he wanted to be invisible, and he was invisible. This was the best evening ever, and it had all started because he'd followed his dad's advice. Hang on, why had his dad told him to go downstairs...?

He asked the clock if his dad had ever experienced the magic. He couldn't believe the answer. His dad was the only one who knew about the clock and he wanted Paul to discover it, but he didn't want to push him to do it. He'd worked with the clock and come up with a plan that would let him try something new and have lots of fun. The only thing was that they couldn't tell his mum, not just yet anyway!

That night, Paul slept and dreamt like never before, all the while thinking about the magical clock he could visit whenever he wanted. He also told himself that he'd have to give his dad a big hug and let him know how much fun he'd had. He could even ask him what things he'd done with the clock's magic over all these years.

It just goes to show what can happen when someone lets you discover something amazing...

DISCLAIMER

This book contains opinions and ideas of the author and is meant to teach the reader informative and helpful knowledge while due care should be taken by the user in the application of the information provided. The instructions and strategies are possibly not right for every reader and there is no guarantee that they work for everyone. Using this book and implementing the information/recipes therein contained is explicitly your own responsibility and risk. This work with all its contents, does not guarantee correctness, completion, quality or correctness of the provided information. Misinformation or misprints cannot be completely eliminated.

Printed in Great Britain
by Amazon